Abby's Adventures
EARTH DAY
...and the Recycling Fashionista!

written by
Suzanne Ridolfi

illustrated by
Dawn Griffin

Eifrig Publishing LLC
Berlin   Lemont

Published by Eifrig Publishing,
PO Box 66, 701 Berry Street, Lemont, PA 16851, USA
Knobelsdorffstr. 44, 14059 Berlin, Germany.

For information regarding permission, write to:
Rights and Permissions Department,
Eifrig Publishing,
PO Box 66, 701 Berry Street, Lemont, PA 16851, USA.
permissions@eifrigpublishing.com, +1-888-340-6543

Library of Congress Cataloging-in-Publication Data
 Ridolfi, Suzanne
Abby's Adventures: Earth Day ... and the Recycling Fashionista/
by Suzanne Ridolfi, illustrated by Dawn Griffin

p. cm.

Paperback: ISBN 978-1-936172-15-3
Hard cover: ISBN 978-1-936172-37-5

[1. Environment – Juvenille Fiction. 2. Self-image – Juvenille Fiction.]

I. Griffin, Dawn, ill. II. Title: Earth Day ... and the Recycling Fashionista

15 14 13 12 2011
5 4 3 2 1

Printed by Jostens in March 2011 on FSC-certified 60% PCW recycled paper. ∞

This special dedication goes out to Lee Duffy, my mother. She taught me unconditional love, empathy, and kindness by example. She is a remarkable lady. I am blessed to have her in my life.

S. R.

"Good morning class and welcome to the beginning of our **Earth Day Celebration**," said Mrs. Cranbrickle.

"This week we will be preparing for our very special celebration. Does anyone know **why** we celebrate Earth Day?" she asked.

"Is it the earth's **birthday?**" asked Abby. Peter Wendell snickered.

"No, but that is a good guess," said Mrs. Cranbrickle.

"Earth Day celebrates how **wonderful** our earth is and what **we** can do to keep it that way."

"The earth is very large, but we are running out of safe places to put our trash. We must find ways to **conserve** and **recycle** to help keep our earth clean."

"What can we do? We're just **kids**," said Ryan.

"We can all help, no matter how **old** or **young** we are," said Mrs. Cranbrickle.

"Class, please take a seat on the carpet. Every morning this week we will be watching videos and reading books about the earth—about things like air pollution, the enormous island of trash we have created in the Pacific Ocean, and the plight of the polar bears, but also about planting trees and gardens, conservation, and recycling."

Mrs. Cranbrickle seemed excited to get started. "We'll think about all the things you and I can do to protect our planet."

"Your Earth Day project is to do some creative environmental thinking of your own to find more ways that you can help make a difference."

"You will all get a chance to present your projects to the class. Then on Earth Day, we'll all get to help prepare the **school garden** to celebrate. When it's your turn to plant your **handful of seeds**, you can share with the class your **Earth Day promises**—promises to help care for the earth."

After the first video was over, the class had already begun to come up with some fun **ideas.**

"Oh, I have a great idea," beamed Abby.

"Oh no!" said Ryan. "She has that look again. Remember how well your last idea to fix Nick's lacrosse stick went?"

ABBY!

"I still think it looked better," exclaimed Abby.

"And how about your **great** idea to transform your dad's shampoo into **pink bubble bath**," recalled Monica.

"Okay, that was not my best idea. It needed some work," said Abby.

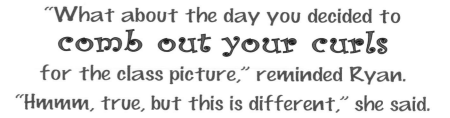

"What about the day you decided to **comb out your curls** for the class picture," reminded Ryan. "Hmmm, true, but this is different," she said.

"I'm going to make the **perfect dress** out of **recycled plastic bottles**," she said with a smile.

10

On their walk home from school that afternoon, Ryan asked, "Do you **really** think we kids can do anything that can make our earth a *better place?*"

They noticed Mrs. Whittaker's yard as they passed by. It had not been cared for since her husband had become ill last fall.

"Are **you** thinking what **I'm** thinking?" asked Abby.

"Meet you here tomorrow after school."

The next day, they asked Mrs. Whittaker if they could help spruce up her yard. They collected *trash* and raked old *leaves*. Underneath them they found tulips trying to break out of the ground. They made a COMPOST site in the corner of the yard.

Mrs. Whittaker was so thankful that she brought them out cookies and lemonade.

At the end of the afternoon, they were proud of the work they had accomplished.

That evening, Abby began working on her own class project.

Abby loved playing *dress up.* She thought she had every type of dress she could imagine.

She had a sequin dress, a dress covered in flowers, she had a velvet dress, a satin dress, and even a suede cowgirl dress with fringe, but she did not yet have a plastic bottle dress. She was so excited.

On Friday, the children were eager to share their projects with the class.

Jimmy made a **magazine rack** out of cereal boxes.

Monica decorated some **burlap bags** for her mother to take along when she went shopping.

Ryan turned old soup cans into **desk organizers** for pens and pencils.

Margaret decorated a large **plastic bin for composting** in her back yard.

"Abby, what have **you** brought in?" asked Mrs. Cranbrickle.

"I need Ryan and Monica's help," replied Abby. The three stepped outside the classroom.

"I'm **afraid** to ask what it is," said Ryan.

Abby slipped on her dress made of large **plastic soda bottles** filled with **pink boas**, fastened together with white ribbon with pink hearts at her neck. Her arms were squeezed through two trimmed 2-liter bottles and were **sticking straight out.**

"What do you think?" she asked.

"Well, I have never seen anything quite like it," said Ryan.

16

"Here comes Abby," he said, as she tried to fit through the door.
"On the count of three, push!" she called out to Ryan and Monica.
"This can't end well," said Ryan pushing with all his might.

Abby **barreled** through the doorway, losing one bottle, which she promptly **slipped** upon, sending her **gliding** across the floor into several other projects and ending up on Mrs. Cranbrickle's desk.

Abby popped up and said, "I'm okay," in a small voice.

"Abby, may I speak with you after class," sighed Mrs. Cranbrickle.

"I just wanted to make a **dress** out of something recycled," Abby said sadly.

"While I appreciate your inner **fashionista**, dear, I think I may have an even **better** idea," said Mrs. Cranbrickle.

"Let's go see **Mrs. Fishman** over in the music room. Her husband works at the **recycling center**, and I think that they might be able to help us out."

After school on Wednesday, Mrs. Fishman brought
Abby and her mother over to visit Mr. Fishman at work.

Abby toured the plant and learned how the
plastic bottles that we put out for collection are first
sorted, chopped up, and washed. Then the plastic
pieces are chopped again to make small flakes.
The flakes are made into even smaller pellets, and the pellets
are then melted down and extruded through a sieve to make
spaghetti-like fibers.

These can then be woven into
all kinds of new fabrics.

It was amazing!

Abby's mother bought her a large piece of recycled-bottle fleece at the recycling center's shop.

Together, Abby and her mother sewed **two** lovely dresses, one for **Abby** and one for her **doll**.

"Abby, dear, I am proud of you for **not giving up**. I know you were **sad** when the other kids laughed at your project, but sometimes it takes **more than one try** to get it right. You should **believe** in yourself. **I do**," smiled Mother.

Next week it was
finally time for the class's
**Earth Day
celebration.**

"Class, Abby has worked
on a new project,"
said Mrs. Cranbrickle.

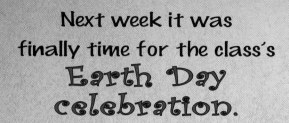

"What is it this time?"
asked Peter Wendell.
"A **shoebox** hat?"

The class laughed.

Abby said proudly,

"I'm wearing it.

My dress is made from recycled **plastic bottles**—about 20, I think—that were melted down and made into new material."

The class looked **surprised.**

Abby told the class about everything she had learned at the recycling factory and passed her **doll** around, who was also wearing the dress she had made from the recycled-plastic fleece.

"The material is so **soft**," said Monica.

"It is really cool, Abby," smiled Ryan. "It sure doesn't **feel** like a **bottle**!"

"Buying **recycled** products is something you can talk to your parents about to help **preserve** our earth. Nice job, Abby," smiled Mrs. Cranbrickle.

Now class, everyone get your cup of seeds so we can plant our garden and make our Earth Day promises," said Mrs. Cranbrickle.
"Let's all promise to make a cleaner earth!"

Dear Journal,
Not all great ideas work out as you hope. Don't give up, even if some kids make you feel sad.
Keep trying, ask for help.
Believe in yourself.
I am a great fashion designer, and I can change the world.
Abby

The End

" Abby takes her young readers on a delightful journey through life lessons on her way to building a healthy self-esteem. This terrific series of books highlights the importance of working through challenging situations towards developing a sense of personal value and accomplishment."

- Dr. Theresa R. Wright, Clinical Psychologist

" A smile sneaks across my face every time I just look at the book, because I know I'm about to meet a spunky, silly example of a great character for girls. She helps us see that self-esteem is built by being open to life's adventures, and my 8-year-old can't wait to see what adventure Abby goes on next!"

- Jess Weiner, author & self-esteem expert

" Abby's Adventures are about the adventures we all have as kids and parents and how the little moments can offer lessons that last a lifetime. Suzanne Ridolfi's stories and Dawn Griffin's illustrations perfectly capture the myriad emotions of childhood -- angst and enthusiasm, triumph and trepidation, whimsy and wonder."

-Brad Herzog, author of "S is for Save the Planet," "P is for Putt," and other books

Our goal is to help each child to realize

that no matter how difficult

growing up may seem,

"It's okay to be me!"

It's okay to be me!

More of Abby's Adventures:
Picture Day ... and the Missing Tooth
Dance Recital ... and the Case of Ballerina-Itis
Freckle Face ... and the Drama Queen

Visit Abby for fun and more green ideas,

including the recycled fleece Abby doll, at

www.abbysfanclub.com!

Make your own Earth Day promises:

I promise to

Feel free to copy and distribute this page to create a tree of promises together with your friends, classmates, and family! Fill in your promises along the veins of the leaf, cut it out, and share your ideas for how you can join in to make a better world!

Believe in yourself, and YOU CAN CHANGE THE WORLD!